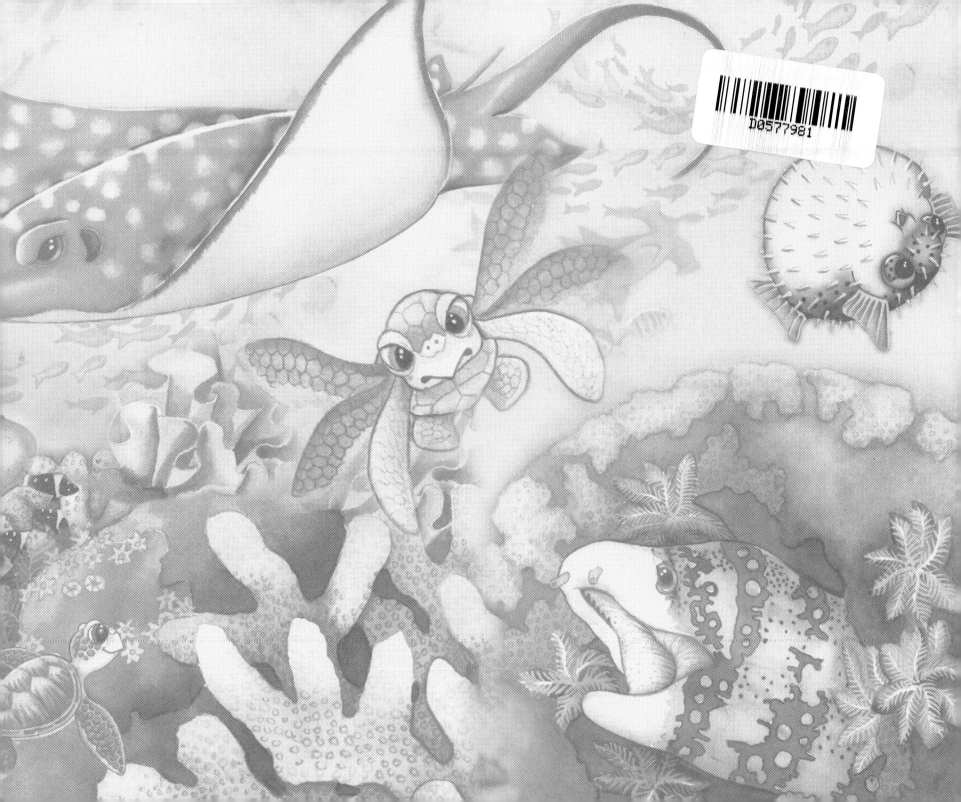

Dedicated to Trevor –

With love and aloha,
Your Aunty Tammy

Published and distributed by

ISLAND HERITAGE
P U B L I S H I N G

99-880 IWAENA STREET, AIEA, HAWAII 96701-3202
PHONE: (808) 487-7299 • Fax: (808) 488-2279
EMAIL: hawaii4u@islandheritage.com

ISBN#: 0-89610-327-7
First Edition, Second Printing - 2000

Baby Honu Saves The Day

Written and Illustrated by Tammy Yee

ISLAND HERITAGE

Baby Honu was a tiny turtle. His sparkling eyes were as round as black pearls. His dark green shell was shaped like Pele's tears. And his flippers were as graceful as a gull's wings, helping him glide with ease through the deep blue water.

But Baby Honu was very shy and very careful. There were many creatures in the sea that were much bigger than he. After all, he was just a little green sea turtle.

"How I wish I were as big and strong as Koholā the whale," thought Baby Honu. "Then I could make a real difference."

3

One day, as Baby Honu was nibbling on some sea grass, he heard a distressful cry. Mama Nai'a was swimming frantically, calling for her keiki. When she saw Baby Honu, she swam over and began to weep.

4

"Oh, little Honu, you must help me," cried Mama Nai'a. "My baby was playing in the shallows when a great wave washed her up onto the beach. Now she is trapped on the sand, and she can't find her way back to the sea!"

"I am just a little turtle," said Baby Honu as he climbed aboard Mama Nai'a's snout, "but I'll see what I can do." Together, they swam to the shore.

5

There, on the sandy beach, they spied Keiki Nai'a. The poor little dolphin wiggled and waggled. She flipped and she flopped. But try as she might, she could not find her way back to the ocean.

Baby Honu climbed up beside her. The poor little turtle pushed and pulled. He huffed and he puffed. But try as he might, he could not move Keiki Nai'a.

"Stay here, little Nai'a, and don't be frightened," soothed Baby Honu. "I will get some help." And back into the sea he went.

The first creature that Baby Honu came upon
was Koholā, the humpback whale.

"Oh, great Koholā, little Keiki Naiʻa is stranded on the beach. Perhaps you are big enough to help her back to sea," pleaded Baby Honu.

"It is true that I am mighty," answered Koholā. "But even I can do nothing for a stranded dolphin. It is the way of the ocean." And off swam the whale.

9

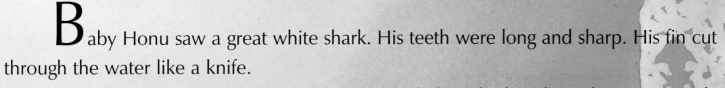

Baby Honu saw a great white shark. His teeth were long and sharp. His fin cut through the water like a knife.

"Oh, terrible Manō, little Keiki Naiʻa is stranded on the beach. Perhaps you are fierce enough to help her back to sea," cried Baby Honu.

"It is true that I am terrifying," shrugged Manō. "But even I can do nothing to help Keiki Naiʻa. It is the way of the ocean." And off swam the shark.

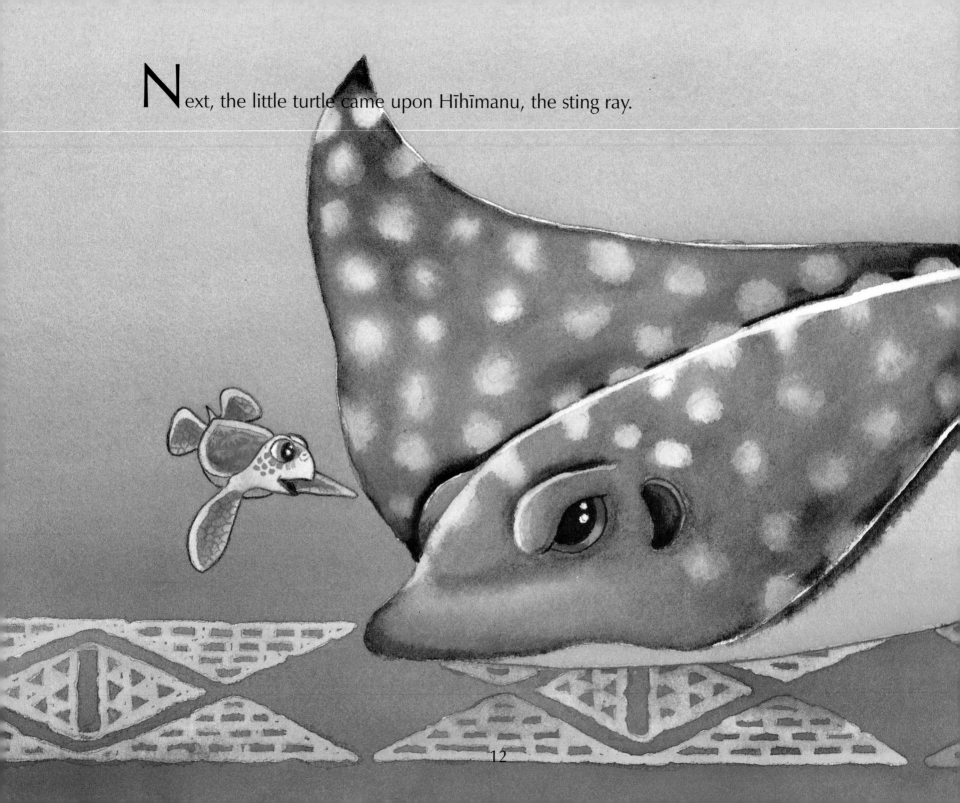

Next, the little turtle came upon Hīhīmanu, the sting ray.

"Oh, Hīhīmanu, with your swift, barbed tail. Keiki Naiʻa is stranded on the beach. Perhaps you are quick enough to help her back to sea," begged Baby Honu.

"It is true that my tail is as fast as lightning," answered Hīhīmanu. "But even I can do nothing to help Keiki Naiʻa. It is the way of the ocean." And off swam the ray.

Poor Baby Honu was desperate. Just then, he saw Kōkala, the porcupinefish.
"Oh, Kōkala, with your long, sharp spines. Keiki Naiʻa is stranded on the beach.
Perhaps you are prickly enough to help her back to sea," pleaded Baby
Honu.

"It is true that I am spiny," sighed Kōkala. "But even I can do
nothing to help the little dolphin. It is the way of the ocean."
And off swam the porcupinefish.

Baby Honu spied Pūhi, the eel, poking his head out of his den. Delicate featherdusters framed the entrance to his home in the coral reef.

"Oh, brave Pūhi, with your jagged teeth," called Baby Honu. "Keiki Naiʻa is stranded on the beach. Perhaps you are bold enough to bring her back to sea!"

"It is true that I am fearless," said Pūhi. "But why bother? Even I can do nothing to help Keiki Naiʻa. Give up, little turtle. It is the way of the ocean." And Pūhi drew back further into his den.

Baby Honu was distraught. Koholā, the whale would not help him. Manō the shark would not help him. Hīhīmanu the stingray would not help him. Kōkala the porcupinefish would not help him. And now, Pūhi the eel would not help him. He was just a tiny turtle. What was he to do?

"Don't give up," said a wee voice. "We can all make a difference."

"Who is it?" asked Baby Honu. He whirled about, but saw no one.

"Down here," said the voice.

Baby Honu peered down and saw a teeny creature on the reef. Dainty yellow tentacles bloomed from a small dimple in the coral, and waved in the current.

"Here I am," it called. "I am a coral polyp. I am tiny, but I am important. My friends and I have built this magnificent reef for all the creatures of the sea to enjoy."

Baby Honu could scarcely believe it. Could this tiny animal have built this great reef? Could a little turtle really make a difference? But what could he do?

Baby Honu saw the featherduster worms lining the entrance to Pūhi's burrow, and he had an idea. He began to fan the feathery creatures with his little fins. Soon the featherdusters were swaying back and forth, back and forth.

18

Deep within Pūhi's den came a deep and slow rumble. The reef began to tremble. Still, Baby Honu kept fanning. Back and forth went the featherdusters. From deep inside, Baby Honu heard a chuckle. Then, a chortle. And finally, a rocking, rollicking, belly-aching, side-splitting, "HA HA HA HA, HOO HOO HOO HOO!"

Tickled by the featherdusters, Pūhi shot out of his burrow with such a loud guffaw that he barreled into Kōkala, the porcupinefish.

WHOOSH, WHOOSH, WHOOSH, WHOOSH! Kōkala was so startled that he GULPED and GULPED and GULPED enough sea water to make himself fat and round and prickly! The frightened puffer tumbled right into . . . sleeping Hīhīmanu!

22

"YOWCH!" cried Hīhīmanu, and he SNAPPED his barbed tail through the water . . . striking fearsome Manō on the tender snout!

24

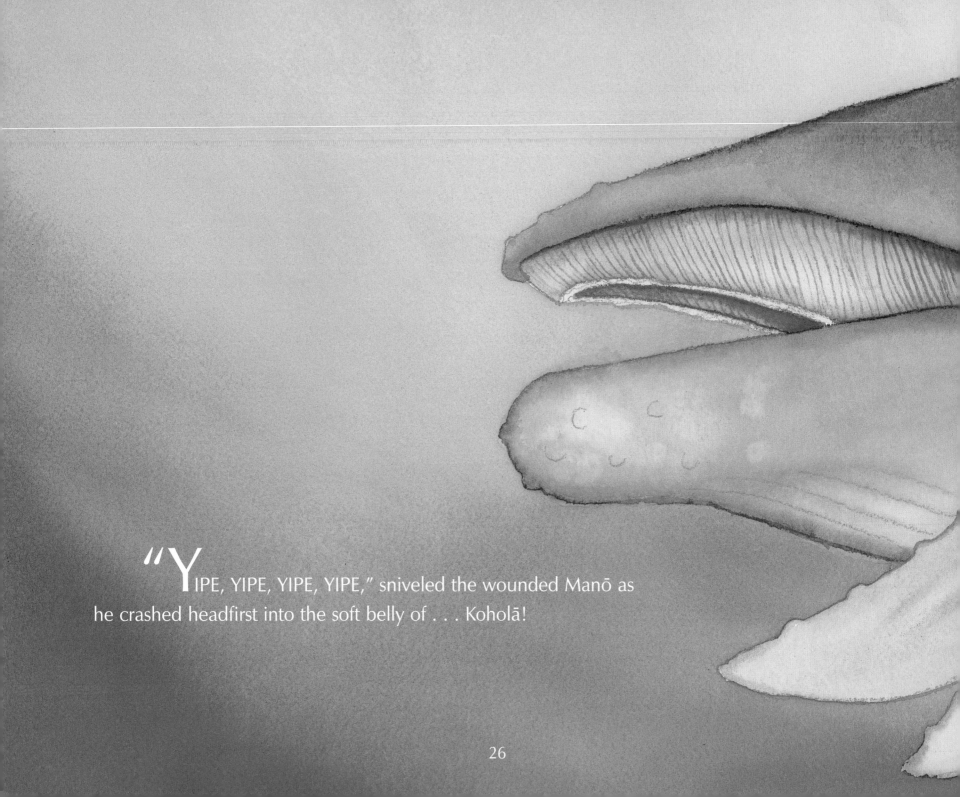

"YIPE, YIPE, YIPE, YIPE," sniveled the wounded Manō as he crashed headfirst into the soft belly of . . . Koholā!

"O_{OOF}!" Poor Koholā was so surprised that he JUMPED clear out of the water and landed in such a tremendous belly flop, that a great wave washed ashore . . .

. . . and carried little Keiki Nai'a back to sea!

Mama Nai'a was so relieved! Her baby dolphin was safe and sound, and all because of a tiny turtle who didn't think he could make a difference.

And Baby Honu never, ever, doubted himself again!

33

GLOSSARY

Hīhīmanu: Stingrays are carnivorous relatives of sharks that feed along the sea floor. They have venomous spines at the base of their long tails.

Honu: Green sea turtles are threatened marine turtles that breed and nest in the remote Northwestern Hawaiian Islands. In the late spring and summer, female turtles clamber ashore to lay 50 to 200 leathery, Ping-Pong ball sized eggs. Two months later, the hatchlings must dig themselves out of their sandy nests and make their way past hungry ghost crabs and seabirds as they scramble to the ocean.

Keiki: Child

Koholā: Humpback whales arrive in Hawai'i each winter to mate and calve. Humpbacks feed by circling around schools of krill (small shrimp-like animals) and creating "nets" of bubbles to entrap their meal. They then swim through the cloud of krill, taking in huge gulps of food which they strain from the water using plates of baleen suspended from the roofs of their mouths.

Kōkala: The porcupinefish is found in tropical waters, where it uses its powerful beak to devour urchins, mollusks, and shellfish. When threatened, it will gulp enough water to inflate itself into a spiny globe, making itself very unpalatable!

Manō: Sharks are prominent in Hawaiian mythology. There are many tales in Hawai'i of supernatural sharks who could transform themselves into human form. Sharks were also common as 'aumākua, or Hawaiian ancestral gods, who could protect a person from shark attacks and guide sailors on long ocean voyages.

Nai'a: Dolphins are intelligent, playful, and social mammals found throughout the Hawaiian Islands. They are well-known for feats of loyalty and devotion toward the members of their pod. A baby bottlenose dolphin, like Keiki Nai'a, learns early to recognize its mother's whistle.

Pele's tears: Pele is the legendary Volcano Goddess, believed to reside on Kīlauea Volcano on the Island of Hawai'i. During eruptions, great fountains of fiery lava sometimes spew fine glassy threads, called Pele's hair. Pele's tears are tear-drop shaped beads that have broken off from the ends of these filaments.

Pūhi: Moray eels are familiar creatures common on Hawaiian reefs. They live in holes and crevices in the reef, where they hunt for fish, crabs, shrimp, and octopi. Morays rarely venture out of their homes. Although their bite is very painful, they rarely do so unless provoked.

The End